For Scarlet and Gabby (who cannot sit still!)

~ S.S.

For my favorite artist, Sasha Polivar

~ E.E.

tiger tales
5 River Road, Suite 128, Wilton, CT 06897
Published in the United States 2018
Originally published in Great Britain 2018
by Little Tiger Press
Text copyright © 2018 Steve Smallman
Illustrations copyright © 2018 Elina Ellis
ISBN-13: 978-1-68010-099-0
ISBN-10: 1-68010-099-8
Printed in China
LTP/1400/2187/0318

For more insight and activities, visit us at www.tigertalesbooks.com

ITCHY, SCRITCHY, SCRATCHY PANTS!

by
Steve Smallman

Illustrated by
Elina Ellis

Five freezing Vikings went out hiking
Through a sudden snowstorm, wondering what to do.
Well, they'd got into a fight, had their undies set alight,
Now their underpants were tattered and their rears were turning blue!

Ooh, the wind's blowing through my underpants!

"My bottom's cold!" moaned Yop as they found a little shop;
A sign said "Knitted Undies" on the door.
But because it was so cold,
    all the undies had been sold,
And there wasn't any wool
    to knit some more!

We're DOOMED!

But the undies lady said, "At the summit of Mount Dread,
There's a Yeti who's mysterious and clever.
So if you bring me a sack of the fur from off his back,
Then I'll knit you all the warmest undies ever!"

BEST KNITTED UNDIES

THE UNDIES LADY of the MONTH

OUT OF STOCK!

In the Forest of Despair
our brave Vikings met a bear,
And a wolf pack
who rushed over to attack.

Let's get 'em!

Harold gave the wolves a shock
with a well-aimed stinky sock,

And the bear hugged Grim . . .
but Grim just hugged him back!

Ahh! He wants a cuddle!

As the Vikings, out of breath,
rowed across the Sea of Death,
They were swallowed by a massive
monster trout!

So then Helga started

whacking it,

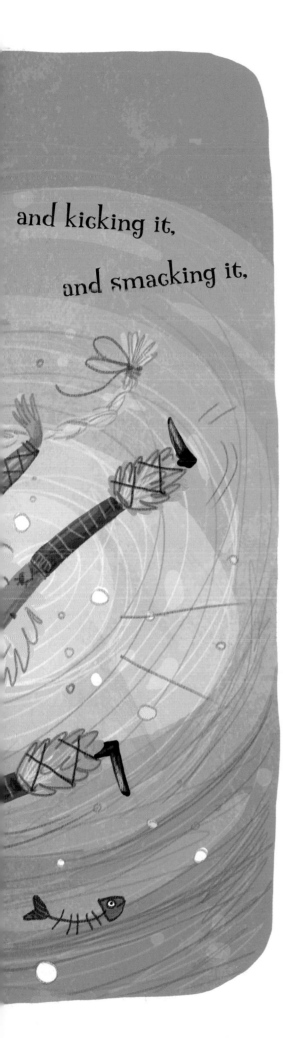

and kicking it,

and smacking it,

Until the fish felt sick
and spat them out!

Well, it's very hard to climb when you're covered in fish slime,
But at last they reached the summit of Mount Dread,
Where they found a fearsome beast (it was 10 feet tall at least!)
And it opened up its massive mouth and said . . .

"Don't be worried! I won't eat you.
I am very pleased to meet you!
People hardly ever come up to my cave!"

Bushy Bigbeard gave a shout,
whipped his Yeti clippers out,
And said, "Come on, gang,
let's give this guy a shave!"

DANGER!
THIN ICE

Then their feet began to slide,
"Ooh, watch out!" the Yeti cried.
"If you fall into Lake Doom it won't be nice."

DANGE
THIN ICE

Well, they did fall in and when
the Yeti pulled them out again,
They were frozen into solid blocks of ice!

Then they heard a mighty roar and the frozen Vikings saw
A huge dragon, who looked down at them and said,
"Viking popsicles! How sweet! You look good enough to eat,
But I think I'll have potato chips instead!"

So the dragon thawed them out
with the fire from his snout,

And the Yeti said, "I do not need a shave!
But if you want some Yeti fluff,
    I've got piles of the stuff.
Look! I keep it all right here inside my cave!"

ive happy Vikings, all quite liking
Riding on a dragon to the Knitted Undies shop;

And when their undies had been knit,
and they tried them and they fit,
Then they paid the undies lady
from the piggy bank of Yop!

Well, the undies were so cozy that their cheeks turned pink and rosy.

Then, "MY BOTTOM IS ALL ITCHY!" Harold cried.

And soon everyone was itching, scratching, jumping 'round, and twitching

As their brand-new pants had YETI FLEAS inside!